The Key
Of Insanity 6

Companion
Of Despair

M.Y. Hauger

Introduction

It seemed like there was nothing that could keep Jayden Williams away from Myah Roxburghe, not even death. She had been relocated several times in an attempt to keep him away from her, but it never worked. Jayden always found her.

It all started when Myah first moved to a neighborhood where her brother, Allen, lived. At first, things seemed to be normal and Myah liked the neighborhood where she lived. She had even found employment at the ice cream shop and the pizzeria that were in the neighborhood.

Then, things took an unexpected turn when Myah discovered an infant that had been abandoned on her porch. She took him in, and she decided to keep him as her own.

The following morning, Myah and Allen took the baby and went to the department store to get the things that were needed for the baby. While they were there, Allen noticed a man who appeared to be watching them. Allen thought it was suspicious, but Myah didn't think anything of it. She figured that it was just a coincidence, and Allen was overreacting. Then the man started showing up at other places where they were. He even made an appearance at the ice cream shop while Myah was working. Shortly afterward, Myah learned that the man had bought the ice cream shop. He suggested that Myah brought her son to work, so they could take turns looking after him. For a while, it worked, but then, things went wrong and Myah ended up quitting the ice cream shop.

Even after Myah had quit, the man, who was actually Jayden, still wouldn't leave her alone. He showed up at her house, even after Myah had quit at the ice cream shop.

Myah decided to leave town in hopes of finding a moment of peace, even if it would've been for a short time. Her attempt had failed because, somehow, Jayden managed to find her.

Even after they had returned, she couldn't get away from him because he decided to stay with her. It seemed like she could find no escape from him. The only time Myah was able to escape him was when she worked at the pizzeria, but even that was short-lived because Jayden had purchased the pizzeria.

When Myah found out that Jayden was the owner of the establishment, she left. There was still no escape for her because he showed up at her house again, and he wouldn't leave. Later, Jayden ended up becoming ill and Myah took care of him while he was in her home. During that time, she developed feelings for him.

Allen, who despised Jayden, saw it as a problem, so he came up with a plan to get his sister away from him. He decided to plan a trip, and he didn't tell his sister the purpose of it. He had planned to have Jayden arrested while they were away, but it didn't work out as he had planned. Jayden showed up at the location where they had been staying. During the night, he would sneak into the beach house where they had been staying, so he could spend the night with Myah. They had gone on several dates together because Jayden had challenged Myah to a round of bowling. Needless to say, Jayden had won, resulting in Myah owing him a kiss and a date. Jayden continued to come up with reasons for the dates not counting so that Myah would have to continue to go out with him.

As time went on, Myah's feelings for Jayden rekindled, and she wanted to spend more time with him. Things took an unpleasant turn when Jayden decided to take Myah and Michael on a boat with the intention of never returning to the area. Allen managed to find them, and he took them from Jayden after he had knocked him out, and then he tried to have him arrested again.

Allen arranged to relocate Myah again to a secluded area. He thought for sure that she would be away from Jayden Williams once and for all. Distance couldn't keep Jayden from her. He showed up in the area where they had been staying. At first, he was upset because he had been abandoned, but then, they had made amends and Jayden stayed in Myah's home with her.

Because of what had happened, Jayden didn't want to be away from Myah any more than he had to be. He also suspected that a man named Albert Hanes had taken interest in Myah. To make things worse, Jayden also found out that Myah shared a dance with King Endymion, whom she had a crush on in the past. Jayden was extremely jealous and wanted no one near her. Albert saw it as a concern, and he also feared for his own life, so he tricked Myah into taking a car ride with him, and they never returned to the area. They ended up in a small town where Myah had to start over once again. Myah was upset with Albert because she loved Jayden, and she didn't want to leave him. She hoped that Jayden would find her. She even wrote a letter to him since she was unable to call him. What she didn't know was that he was already in the area, devising a plan of his own. He was fed up with having his family torn away from him, and he wanted to put a stop to it. Eventually, he took Myah and Michael and hid them in the basement of the local pizzeria that he had purchased.

Because he was hurt and angry, Jayden ended up making Myah miserable. He constantly yelled at her, and he wanted to know her every move. It was like a prison for her. Meanwhile, Albert suspected that something was wrong because Myah had not been around to drop Michael off at his home before she went to work. He decided to stop at her home to see if she was alright. When he realized that she was missing, he contacted Allen, and they teamed up, so they could find Myah and Michael. When they located them, they took them, left the area, and fled to an abandoned house where they hid. The following morning, they were awakened by Jayden, who was pounding on the door before he busted through it, so he could get to Myah once again. Allen and Albert told Myah to take Michael and run. She was reluctant to leave, but then she fled. As she ran, she heard two gunshots. Shortly afterward, she was met by a man who took Myah and Michael away from the area, and they were relocated once again.

There were many things that were unanswered and for a while, she didn't hear anything from anyone. She tried to carry on with her life, even though it was difficult at times. She took an online job, so she could be with her son. Little did she know, her manager ended up being none other than King Endymion, who wanted to help the family in every way possible.

With time, Myah opened up to him, especially after she started receiving strange packages. At first, it had appeared that Jayden Williams had been killed, and Myah was devastated because of it. Then, one day, while Myah was taking a walk, she spotted Jayden in the area. Even death couldn't keep him from her. It wasn't long after that when he showed up at her home. She kept herself hidden from him, and she even discovered an underwater shelter beneath her home, where she and Michael then stayed. The hiding was short-lived, for Jayden had figured it out. Once again, Myah was trapped by Jayden, who was angry and hurt. At first, she tried to get away from him until he told her that Allen had shot him. Then he showed the wounds to Myah, who broke down in tears at that moment. One of the wounds was on his abdomen, while the other was a chest wound. Jayden told her that the bullets were still there, and he wanted her to remove them. She wanted to take him to the hospital, but he refused to go. Myah reluctantly did as he wanted, but then, he ended up going unconscious while in her arms. She just couldn't let him die, so she dialed the emergency number, but for some reason, it was Endymion who was on the other end. She explained that Jayden was dying and without hesitation, Endymion came to the rescue, and he healed Jayden. The pain was gone, and the wounds were no longer there.

The following morning, Jayden woke up and realized that the pain and the wounds were gone. He was happy that he was healed. He was even happier that he was back with his family and that his family was growing. At that moment, Jayden felt that it was a new beginning for him and his family, whom he was reunited with once again.

Chapter 1

Even though several hours had passed, since Jayden Williams had awakened, it was still early in the morning, and he didn't feel like moving from the bed. Normally, he would be up early in the morning but at that moment, he just didn't feel like getting up. He just wanted to take in everything that was around him. Jayden sighed as he rested on the bed. He glanced over at the window, and then he looked over at the clock. It seemed as though time was passing slowly, but Jayden didn't mind, in fact, he was glad about it. After all that he had been through, he didn't want to take a single moment for granted.

Jayden reflected on everything that had happened as he rested against Myah whom he had awakened hours ago. He closed his eyes for a moment as she hugged him tightly. More than likely, she was also thinking about things that had taken place recently. Jayden opened his eyes, and then he looked into Myah's eyes for a moment before he gave her a kiss. Then he sighed as he rested against her. He closed his eyes again as he reflected on the things that had happened. What Jayden thought about the most were the things that had taken place during the past several days. It was just a day ago when Jayden was knocking on death's door. He was fully aware of the severity of his condition, yet he refused to give up on finding the ones whom he loved. He knew that his injuries were fatal, but nothing was stopping him from being reunited with his family, even if it would've been for only a moment.

Thankfully, Endymion had shown up after Myah had called for help. He was relieved that Jayden was still alive, and he healed him. It was as though he had never been shot. Endymion made sure that Jayden remained asleep while he was there. He knew that if Jayden knew that he was there, he would be upset, regardless of the fact that Endymion saved his life.

Jayden was not aware of the fact that he had been healed. He just knew that he should've been dead, yet, somehow, he wasn't. As he continued to reflect on the things that had happened, he became amazed at how quickly things had changed. Not long ago, he was fighting for his life. At that moment, he was content as he rested in the arms of the one who he had fallen in love with; the one who he was determined to be with. He was happy with how things were at that moment, and he was even happier that there was no one around who would come between them.

Chapter 2

Several hours had passed and Myah got up and left the room to check on Michael. As she entered the room, she noticed right away that he was awake. She changed him, and then she took him to the bedroom and sat down before she fed him. Jayden glanced at her before he moved closer to her, and then he rested against her. As Myah looked at both of them, she thought about how thankful she was that Jayden was there, and he was alive. It was a miracle that he had survived, and she didn't want to take him for granted. She was also thankful that Michael wouldn't be left fatherless and Jayden would be able to be a part of his life. Jayden looked into her eyes as he spoke.

"You have something on your mind." he said.

"Yes."

"What is it?" Jayden asked.

"I was just thinking about how close you came to dying and…" Myah said.

She fought back tears as she glanced down at Michael. Jayden sat up, and then he hugged Myah tightly as he spoke.

"It's alright, Myah. It's all over now." Jayden said.

"Maybe so, but it wasn't all that long ago when you were fighting for your life."

"Yes, I realize that, however, I think it would be best if we tried to move on from it now."

"Had I known what would've happened, I would've never left."

"Myah, please, try to let it go. It's in the past now." Jayden said.

He gave her a kiss before he took Michael from her. Jayden looked at him and smiled before he gave him a kiss on the forehead. Then he spoke softly to him, just as he had done before. Jayden glanced at Myah as he spoke.

"We're together now. That's what truly matters." Jayden said.

With a smile still on his face, he looked into her eyes before he gave her a kiss.

"I just still can't get over the fact that he shot you. He kept going on about how dangerous and toxic you were, yet he was the one who shot you." Myah said.

"Precisely, and as I said before, I didn't have a weapon. It was obvious that he was trying to kill me."

"You know, the more I think about it, the more disappointed and disgusted I become with him. I couldn't care less if the king would arrest him."

"Kindly leave the king out of it. I could do without hearing about him." Jayden said.

"Sorry. I just figured that he would be upset about what Allen did." Myah said.

Jayden said nothing as he looked at Myah with an unhappy expression on his face.

"Allen was so adamant about having you arrested, yet he should be the one who goes to jail." Myah said.

"It seemed like he would stop at nothing to keep me from you, even if it meant murdering me."

"I am so sorry. You were right, and he took it too far. As I look back, I realize that he interfered way more than he should've."

"I don't understand what his problem was. I never did a thing to him, yet he caused trouble for me from day one. What a lot of people don't realize is that I'm hurting. I have a broken heart." Jayden said.

Myah looked at Jayden, who then looked into her eyes with an expression of sorrow on his face. Then Myah glanced at Michael, who was about to fall asleep. She got up and took Michael, so she could put him into his crib. When she returned to the room, Jayden still had a sad expression on his face.

"Myah, I still need you to take care of me." Jayden said.

Myah sat down on the bed, and then Jayden moved close to her, so he could rest against her as she hugged him tightly.

"Even though my physical wounds have healed, there are still emotional wounds that have not healed, and they are painful." Jayden said.

Myah hugged him even tighter.

"I'm a wounded spirit with a broken soul. I need love and care. You have no idea about the things that I've been through. You don't know about the many times that my heart has been shattered. There never seems to be a chance for me to heal. Instead, the wounds become worse." Jayden said.

"I'm so sorry." Myah said.

"Perhaps, with time and the proper care, the wounds could eventually heal."

"Do you want to talk about it?"

"I feel so unloved. Why does nobody want me?"

"I love you, and I want you."

"Do you? It wasn't so long ago when you were trying to escape me."

"It was because I was afraid."

"Why?"

"You seemed so upset."

"That was because I was hurting. That's all the more reason for you to stay with me."

"But I do love you."

"My father never wanted me. He told me so. He told me that he hated me. He tried to kill me." Jayden said.

At that moment, Myah's eyes welled up with tears as she hugged him tightly.

"I don't know why he didn't love me, but he never did. I asked for nothing from him except his love and acceptance, but he couldn't give me that. He wouldn't." Jayden said.

"It's terrible that your father would be so unkind to you. I can't imagine how painful it must have been for you."

"Thankfully, my mother loved me, but unfortunately, she passed away when I was very young. After that, my father became even worse."

"How tragic."

"I was only three when she passed away. I know that my father was devastated by what happened. I wanted to comfort him, but he lashed out at me. He blamed me for what happened to her, and then he beat me. He tried to strangle me, but something must have happened that caused him to stop. I don't remember what it was."

"What happened to your mother?" Myah asked.

"Nobody knows. All I remember was that there was a strange bite on her. Nobody saw what happened." Jayden said.

At that moment, he broke down and wept.

"I'm so sorry. I wish I knew how to help you." Myah said.

"But you already are helping me."

"I don't feel like I'm doing much for you."

"You're here with me. You're willing to listen to me and take care of me. You're helping more than you realize."

"I'm so sorry about your parents. That's so sad."

"Even now, it's difficult for me. As for my father, I still don't understand why he hated me so much. I don't understand why he acted as he did. I just know that it broke my heart. It still hurts. The worst thing about it is that there will never be a way to resolve it."

"Is he still around?" Myah asked.

"To be honest, I don't know. I haven't seen him, so I assume that he must have either left the area or he died, otherwise, he would probably be still trying to kill me."

"Thankfully, his attempt had failed. It's terrible that your own father would do that to you."

"I know, nevertheless, that's how it is." Jayden said.

Myah squeezed Jayden tightly, and then she looked into his eyes before she closed her eyes and gave him a kiss. Then she hugged him tightly once again. Myah felt sad for Jayden and as she continued to think about the things that he had told her, she hugged him even tighter.

"It seems that my entire life has been a series of tragedies, but you see, it's you and Michael that keep me going. It's because of the two of you that I didn't give up." Jayden said.

He then looked at Myah for a moment before he continued to speak.

"I know that people say that there's something wrong with me, and the truth is, they're right. It's my heart. It's been bruised and broken continually by people who were supposed to love me, but for some reason, they chose not to care. Did you know that a person can die of a broken heart?" Jayden said.

Myah hugged him even tighter.

"Hug me tighter, Myah. Never let me go." Jayden said.

Myah hugged him even tighter.

"You have no idea how much I need this. I need to feel like I'm wanted. I want to know without a doubt that I'm loved." Jayden said.

"I love you." Myah said.

"I love you, too, but unfortunately, words are not enough."

"What would it take for it to be enough?" Myah asked.

Jayden said nothing as he looked at her with sad eyes.

"I want to make you feel better." Myah said.

"Do you?"

"Yes. What will make you feel better?" Myah said.

Jayden didn't respond, as he continued to look at her with a sad expression on his face. Myah gently touched the side of his face before she gave him a kiss. Then she ran her fingers through his hair, even as he rested against her.

"I've lost so much in the past. I don't want to go through it again. I don't want to lose anyone else. It's too much for me to endure." Jayden said.

He then looked into Myah's eyes.

"You said that you want to make me feel better." Jayden said.

"Yes." Myah said.

Jayden then closed his eyes as he gave Myah a kiss.

"I must tell you that it's going to take some time, but, perhaps, with time, and the right amount of love and care, the wounds may eventually heal." Jayden said.

"Whatever it is that you need me to do, I'll do it."

"Do you mean that?"

"Yes." Myah said.

Jayden then gave Myah a kiss, and then he hugged her tightly as he spoke.

"Thank you. I truly feel that you will help me through the heartache that I've been dealing with." he said.

He then closed his eyes as he hugged her even tighter. Then he spoke softly into her ear.

"I love you."

Chapter 3

Several hours had passed and Myah was about to get up when Jayden took hold of her hand. She glanced at Jayden, who had a sad expression on his face.

"Stay here with me." Jayden said.

"But I'm not going anywhere. I was going to check on Michael." Myah said.

Jayden then let go of Myah's hand.

"Hurry back." he said.

Myah gave Jayden a kiss before she got up and left the room to check on Michael. It wasn't long until Myah had returned to the room. When she approached the bed, she sat down beside Jayden, who moved closer to her before he rested against her.

"He's still asleep." Myah said.

"Whenever he does wake up, you can bring him here so that I can spend time with him." Jayden said.

"How are you feeling? Are you doing alright?" Myah asked.

"I don't know. I am happy with the way things are right now, but I can't get over the fact that I almost died."

"I know. It was terrible."

"Yes, and it has me thinking, and I realize that I don't want to take a single moment for granted."

"That's understandable."

"We should spend as much time together as possible."

"I agree." Myah said.

"I don't want to be apart from you, Myah. I want to be near you all the time. I want nothing to come between us."

"At this point, I don't think that there is anything else that could come between us."

"I'd like to think that, but for some reason, there always seems to be something or someone that tries to tear us apart."

"I really don't think that you need to worry. I haven't heard from Allen or Albert." Myah said.

"That's probably because they're hiding. Since they're fugitives, they're not going to want to be found." Jayden said.

"I should probably check on Michael." Myah said.

She got up and left the room to check on Michael, who was awake. She took him out of the crib and took him to the bedroom, where she took care of him. Myah and Jayden spent time with him until he had fallen asleep, and then Myah took him back to his room and put him into his crib. Then she left the room and went back to her room and sat down beside Jayden.

"I'm hoping that you'll stay here with me for the entire day." Jayden said.

"But I'm not going anywhere." Myah said.

"I realize that, but what I meant was that I want you to stay here in the room with me the entire day. I realize that you would have to step out now and then to take care of Michael, but aside from that, you could stay here with me." Jayden said.

Myah glanced at Jayden, who looked at her with sad eyes.

"Please, Myah. We should try to spend every moment together that we possibly can." Jayden said.

"Alright."

"Thank you, Myah." Jayden said.

He moved over closer to her, and then he gave her a kiss before he rested against her.

"It means a lot to me that you're willing to do this for me. Every moment that we have together is precious, and we should not take it for granted, nor should we waste it." Jayden said.

He then took hold of Myah's hand, even as he rested against her.

"I love you so much." Jayden said.

He then kissed her hand.

"You have no idea how much I need this. I spent most of my life feeling unloved. The few people who did care about me were taken from me. It's very painful for me." Jayden said.

"I'm so sorry."

"I need you to take care of me. Even though my physical wounds have healed, I'm still hurting." Jayden said.

He then looked at Myah again, still with a sad expression on his face. Myah's heart sank as she looked into Jayden's sad eyes, and she hugged him tightly.

Myah spent most of the day taking care of Jayden. She only left the room whenever she absolutely needed to because Jayden wanted her to stay in the room with him the entire day. As time went on, Myah started to grow tired from taking care of both Jayden and Michael.

Finally, during the early evening, Jayden drifted off to sleep. Myah ended up turning in early after she had finished taking care of Michael because she was tired from the busy day that she had.

Chapter 4

Myah continued to take care of both Michael and Jayden. She kept busy during the day taking care of both of them. Most of the time was spent with Jayden, since Michael was still napping frequently. Even while Myah took care of Michael, she brought him into the room because that was what Jayden wanted. He wanted to spend time with his son, so they could bond with one another.

Then, one day, while Jayden wasn't paying attention, Endymion showed up with food and other things, and he quickly put Jayden to sleep, so he wouldn't know that he was there.

"Hello, Myah. How have you been?" Endymion said.

"I've been alright. I've been keeping busy." Myah said.

Endymion put the things that he had brought down before he made his way over to Myah and took Michael.

"I sort of figured that. I told you that he would be a handful. Somehow, I knew that he would want lots of attention, even though his wounds have been healed." Endymion said.

"I know, but he says that he still has emotional wounds that have not healed."

"I also figured that he would play that card."

"He told me about some of the things from the past."

"Right, and although there's no doubt that he's hurting, I want to make sure that he doesn't wear you down. You don't need that right now. If anything, he should be taking care of you, after all, you're carrying his babies."

"I understand that. Perhaps he just needs time."

"Right, but how much time?" Endymion asked.

Myah didn't respond.

"Please, don't get upset with me. I just don't want you to become overwhelmed because of him. I get that you love him and I already knew that he would be a handful, but he pursued you. He stopped at nothing just to be with you, and the two of you chose to be together. At some point, he's going to have to do his part." Endymion said.

He looked at Michael, and then he smiled as he spoke to him. Then changed him and he washed his hands before he picked him up again and started to sing to him. When Michael was about to fall asleep, Endymion put him into his crib. Then he took the things that he had brought and put them away.

"I wish you could stay. I miss having you around." Myah said.

Endymion looked at Myah with an expression of concern on his face.

"You know that I can't do that. I have so much to do, and there are many who I need to take care of. Besides, I don't think that it would be a good idea." he said.

"It's too bad you had to put him to sleep. He still doesn't know that you healed him."

"Don't tell him. It's best if he doesn't know."

"But why? You did a good thing. You're his hero."

"You and I both know that if he knew that I was here, he'd be upset. He'd be wanting to pick a fight, and frankly, I don't feel like fighting. I just want to make sure everyone is alright."

"I see that, and I appreciate that."

"Just promise me that you won't let him overwhelm you. If he gets to be too much for you to handle, let me know. I'll figure something out. In the meantime, I should probably go." Endymion said.

He turned and as he was about to leave, Myah spoke.

"Endymion." she said.

Endymion turned and looked at her.

"I…" Myah said.

Endymion's expression suddenly became sorrowful as he looked at her.

Myah could see that he was fighting back tears.

“I have to go.” Endymion said.

He then opened the door and walked out. Myah rushed over to the door and opened it, but Endymion was gone. Myah sighed before she went back inside and closed the door.

Chapter 5

Endymion went back to where he had been staying. When he got there, he started to pace the floor. He was both frustrated and heartbroken about the situation with Myah and her family. His heart sank deeper and deeper as he continued to pace the floor while he thought about the situation. Endymion knew that the family was going through a difficult time, and he wanted to help them in every way that he possibly could. Unfortunately, the situation was becoming more and more uncomfortable for him. There were things that he knew that the family wasn't aware that he had knowledge of. Endymion also knew what it was that Myah was going to say to him. He stopped pacing the floor as he cupped his hands to his face. Then he walked over to a chair and sat down.

Endymion hated the complications of the situation, and he did not want trouble, but he still wanted to help Myah and her family as much as possible. As Endymion continued to think about the difficult situation, his heir quietly entered the room. He had an expression of concern on his face as he walked toward Endymion, who then looked at him. When the boy approached him, he looked him in the eyes before he spoke.

"Are you alright?" the boy asked.

"Why do you ask?" Endymion asked.

"You seem upset about something."

"It's complicated."

"Is there anything I can do to help?" the boy asked.

"No, son, but thanks. You're much too young to trouble yourself with such things." Endymion said.

The boy was about to walk away, but then he looked at Endymion before he gave him a hug. Endymion managed to smile as he hugged his heir, and then he spoke.

"Thank you, my child. You're such a good son, and someday, you will make an excellent king."

Chapter 6

Myah was disappointed that Endymion had left so quickly. She wished that he could've stayed a little longer. She missed him when he wasn't there, and it seemed like she was seeing less and less of him.

Myah also realized that Endymion seemed unhappy about something as he left, and it made her feel sad that he was hurting because of it. Myah suspected that Endymion was trying to hide his pain, but she could see it.

Endymion crossed Myah's mind often, and the less she saw of him, the more she thought of him. She tried not to think about him, but the harder she tried, the more she thought about him, and it caused her to feel frustrated.

It has been said that oftentimes, whenever someone falls in love with Endymion, it's difficult to just forget about him and move on. Myah's frustration grew because she had fallen in love with him. What started out as a silly crush became something more, and even though he hardly came around, her feelings for him continued to grow.

Myah wanted it to stop. She wanted to move on, but the feelings continued to grow. Myah felt horrible because of it because she also loved Jayden and her feelings for him also continued to grow. It was Jayden who she wanted to be with.

Jayden could see that something was upsetting Myah, even though he didn't know what it was that was causing her distress. Not knowing the reason behind her frustration, Jayden tried to comfort her. He let her know that whatever it was that was going through, she wouldn't have to deal with it alone. Jayden let her know that he would help her through it, and they'd overcome it together.

Chapter 7

As time went on, Jayden and Myah grew closer. They were happy to be back in each other's lives. Jayden was also happy that Myah was happy to have him back in her life. As for Endymion, he decided that it would be best if he'd come during the night while everyone was asleep. He wanted to continue to help Myah, but at the same time, he didn't want to come between her and Jayden. He knew that she cared about Jayden, so he felt that it was best if he wasn't seen.

Even though he tried to avoid being seen by Myah and Jayden, he still spent time with Michael whenever he was there. He would take care of him while he was there, and when the child fell asleep, Endymion would put him back into the crib before he would leave. He never left a trace, other than the food and the other things that he would bring to supply the family's needs. Afterward, he would go to the home where his heir lived so that he could spend time with him and look after him. Endymion tried to spend more time with his heir whenever he wasn't busy taking care of other things. Sometimes he would take his heir with him, depending on where he would go or what he was planning to do. Endymion and the child had bonded over time, but it made Endymion sad that he couldn't be with him even more.

Late in the night, while his heir was asleep, Endymion thought about Myah's son, Michael. He hoped that he would have a happy childhood. He hoped that he would have a father who would love and care for him, as a father should. He wanted the vicious cycle to

end so that the child's life would not be
destroyed.

Chapter 8

Since Myah no longer had a reason to hide, she hoped that she would be able to get outside for fresh air again. She hoped that she could either take a walk or go for a swim. When she asked Jayden about it, she could see right away that he wasn't thrilled with the idea.

"Is there something wrong?" Myah asked.

"Why can't we just stay inside?" Jayden asked.

"I just thought it would be nice to go outside. Wouldn't it be nice to take a walk or go for a swim?"

"I don't think it's a good idea."

"Why not? Allen and Albert aren't in the area."

"No, but who's to say that someone else wouldn't come along and try to break our family apart?" Jayden said.

"I understand the reason that you'd be reluctant to go outside, but we can't live in fear. What's the fun in that?"

"I've lost so much in the past. I don't want to go through it again."

"Jayden, listen to me. I'm not going anywhere. I told you that there would be no more running. I meant that."

"If it's all the same to you, I'd rather wait. I'd rather play it safe.

Please, don't be upset with me about that." Jayden said.

"I'm not upset. I understand. If you need more time, we'll take more time. Okay?"

"Thank you." Jayden said.

He then hugged Myah before he gave her a kiss.

"I'm glad that you understand the reason that I would rather wait. We don't need to be out there. I'm content being here with you. Are you content being here with me?" Jayden said.

He then looked at Myah with sad puppy dog eyes.

"Of course. I wouldn't have it any other way." Myah said.

Jayden then closed his eyes as he rested against Myah.

"I was beginning to worry about the possibility of you not being satisfied with being here with me." Jayden said.

"It couldn't be further from the truth."

"My heart has been broken in the past by others and by you."

"I'm sorry."

"I realize that, however, I cannot ignore the fact that you had run out on me on several occasions. You abandoned me whenever I needed you most."

"Jayden, you have to believe me whenever I tell you that it wasn't my fault. The first time, Allen didn't tell me that he planned the trip for the purpose of separating us. It was also Allen's idea to move me to the secluded area. It wasn't mine."

"What about when you left me in the boat alone and unconscious? And what about the time when you abandoned me during the night at the secluded area? I was under the impression that you wanted to be with me. We could've had a beautiful thing there." Jayden said.

"It wasn't my fault. Albert tricked me. I had no idea that he wanted to take me away from you. As for the boat incident, you frightened me. Anyway, Allen showed up and knocked you out. I had nothing to do with that, nor did I want him to leave you like that."

"I always knew that Albert was trouble. It's the whole reason that I wanted people to stay away. I never trusted him. As for Allen, he was so adamant about having me arrested when I should've pressed charges against him for harassment and assault. Not once had I ever hit him, but he knocked me out. He wouldn't leave me alone. Then, to top it all off, he tried to murder me. Even then, I didn't want to fight, yet he and Albert both ganged up on me and beat me before Allen shot me. The thing is, I could've taken them both down very easily, but I chose not to. Why? I refrained from fighting them because Allen's your brother. I knew that you were close to him, and I didn't want to upset you."

"I'm so sorry."

"I had every reason to be upset and if I would've fought back, I could've defeated him, and he would've deserved it. He continually caused trouble for us. He kept tearing us apart. That's unacceptable." Jayden said.

Myah could see the pain in his eyes as he fought back tears.

"What about the time whenever we stayed in the basement of the pizzeria?" Jayden asked.

"You were scaring me. You were constantly yelling at me. It was hard to deal with."

"I had every right to be upset. You left me, and you didn't even give me so much as an explanation."

"It wasn't my choice. I told you already that Albert tricked me."

"I needed you, just as I needed you at that abandoned building where I had been shot. I still need you."

"I'm here now. I told you that I wouldn't run anymore."

"But you've done it so many times. I can't help but wonder about whether you're content being here with me."

"I am content with you. I love you. I want to spend my life with you." Myah said.

Jayden then looked into Myah's eyes as he spoke.

"Do you truly mean that?" he asked.

"Yes."

"I want to spend my life with you too." Jayden said.

He then gave Myah a kiss.

"If more time is what you need, I'm okay with that. I understand. I'm content being here with you, and I can wait for whenever you're ready." Myah said.

She then gave him a kiss, and she hugged him tightly. Jayden sighed before he spoke.

"Thank you for understanding. I just don't want anything or anyone to come between us. Now that we're back together, I want us to remain that way."

Chapter 9

Even though Myah wanted to get out to enjoy a walk or a swim, she didn't say anything about it. She didn't want to upset Jayden, since he had made it blatantly clear that he had no desire to go outside. He preferred to stay inside, where he and his family remained hidden in the underwater shelter.

During that time, Jayden sought Myah's attention more and more. He often talked about the pain he was feeling from being abandoned. Myah gave him the attention that he wanted because she wanted to make him feel better.

As time went on, Jayden and Myah grew even closer to one another. With time, Jayden became more active within the home, even though he still wanted to be near Myah all the time.

The two of them worked together to take care of Michael. They also worked together to maintain the home. Jayden decided to set things up, so he could run the businesses that he had purchased without leaving home. He also started thinking about everything that he would need to do in order to prepare for his new arrivals. With each day that passed, he became happier about the thought of his family growing. He thought that his life would finally turn around, and he would eventually overcome the heartaches that he had been dealing with. At that moment, it truly did seem like a new beginning for him and his family, whom he loved.

Chapter 10

As time went on, Myah found herself wanting to get out more and more. For a while, Jayden wasn't okay with the idea. Then, one evening, he decided to meet her halfway. After Michael had fallen asleep, the two of them decided to go for an evening swim. After they had gotten ready, the two of them went outside and swam up until they had gotten to the top. They both exhaled before they glanced around.

"You know, we probably wouldn't need to block the trap door anymore. Even if you would want to remain in the underwater shelter, we could use the trapdoor to go in and out. It would probably be much easier for us." Myah said.

"If that's what you want." Jayden said.

He then gave her a kiss before he hugged her tightly.

"It's a beautiful night." Myah said.

"Yes, it is." Jayden said.

He then smiled as he glanced at Myah's abdomen.

"I see that you're developing a bump. I think it's adorable." he said.

He then kissed Myah's abdomen before he hugged her tightly.

"Let's go for a swim." Jayden said.

He gave her a kiss before the two of them started to swim beneath the moonlight. They stayed close to one another as they swam. Then Jayden took hold of Myah, and then he kissed her before they continued to swim. They stayed out for a little while, and then they went inside through the main house. Jayden walked into the bedroom where the trapdoor was, so he could unblock it. Afterward, he opened the trapdoor and he and Myah went back down to the underwater shelter where they had been staying. Jayden closed and locked the trapdoor before he went down the steps. When they got down to the bottom of the stairs, they kissed before they went into Michael's room to see if he was awake. He was still asleep, so Myah and Jayden went into their room, so they could get out of their wet swimming clothes. Afterward, they both made their way to the bed, and they got onto it before they hugged one another.

"Thank you." Myah said.

"For what?"

“For a great time.”

“It was nice to get out.”

“Maybe we could do it more often.”

“Perhaps.” Jayden said.

He then hugged Myah even tighter before he eventually went to sleep.

Chapter 11

As time went on, Myah and Jayden started to go out more and more. They often went for an evening swim after Michael had fallen asleep. On days when they were unable to go for an evening swim, they would snuggle close to one another, and then they would find a movie to watch.

Then, one day, Myah suggested that they take an evening walk before Michael fell asleep, and then they could go for a swim afterward. Surprisingly, Jayden liked the idea, so after dinner, they put Michael into the stroller, and then they went for a walk.

"I will say that this area is quite different from the other places where you've lived." Jayden said.

"I feel like most of them were different, although this one is more different than any of them."

"I don't plan to make this our permanent residence, although I do believe that this place has potential, particularly the underwater shelter."

"Do you really think so? I mean, it is really nice, however, it doesn't even have a yard for Michael to play in."

"I may have other plans for that place, as well as the pizzerias and ice cream shop. You see, my goal is to become a better businessman than my father ever was."

"Jayden, you don't need to compete with him, nor do you need to prove anything. It sounds like you're already a better man than he'll ever be."

"Everyone sang praises about him as a businessman."

"Does it really matter?" Myah asked.

Jayden didn't respond as he glanced at Myah with an unhappy expression on his face.

"How about we don't talk about your father anymore. He doesn't matter. To me, you're the one that matters. I couldn't care less about him." Myah said.

"Fair enough." Jayden said.

He then glanced around.

"Have you ever wondered about the places in this area? I know that there's a small shop. I've been in it. Of course, they didn't have what I was looking for." Jayden said.

He then glanced at her.

"What were you looking for?" Myah asked.

"I think you know the answer to that." Jayden said.

"Do I?"

"I was looking for you, Myah." Jayden said.

He then stopped, and he took hold of Myah, so she would stop.

"I knew that you were close by. To be honest, I think I may have seen you as I was leaving the shop. As I told you before, I'll always find you." Jayden said.

He then gave Myah a kiss.

"I'm glad that you found me. I was happy to know that you were still alive. I was devastated when I got those packages in the mail."

"I sent them to you. I wasn't sure if I would survive, and I wanted you to know the truth. I wanted you to know what happened. That's the reason I sent the shirt to you. I sent you my belongings because I wanted you to have them. As for the photographs, I wanted to show you that I was being truthful when I told you that I'm Michael's father."

"Message received."

"Thankfully, I managed to survive long enough to find you. I wanted to be with you, even if it was for the final moments of my life." Jayden said.

At that moment, Myah's eyes welled up with tears.

"It's alright, Myah. I'm here now. I didn't mean to upset you." Jayden said.

He then hugged her tightly.

"I love you so much." Myah said.

"I love you too. You have no idea how much it means to me to hear you say those words."

"I feel like I can't speak them enough. You almost died. I could've lost you."

"But I'm here now, so try not to think about that."

"Sometimes it's hard not to." Myah said.

"I realize that, but what good does it do to dwell on it? It's not good for you or the babies." Jayden said.

He then gave Myah a kiss.

"Perhaps we should continue our walk." Jayden said.

"You're right." Myah said.

The two of them moved on as they walked through the village. As they walked, they spotted a few small shops and two small diners. Myah started thinking about all the times when she and Jayden went on dates together while they were on their mini vacation.

"You're thinking about something." Jayden said.

"Maybe."

"What is it?" Jayden asked.

"I was thinking about all the dates that didn't count."

"Oh."

"Actually, I'm kind of glad it happened."

"You are?"

"Yeah."

"It would've been better had your brother not interfered."

"I know, but maybe we can pick up where we left off. This time, he's not around to intervene."

"As nice as that all sounds, I was hoping that we had moved past all that, after all, in several months, you'll be giving birth to two new babies."

"I see what you're saying, and I agree with you, but it doesn't mean we can't still enjoy a nice evening together."

"I don't plan for us to stay here for too long. I have a home where I want to take you."

"It doesn't matter where we are. We could still enjoy a nice evening, whether it's here or in some other neighborhood. It doesn't matter as long as we're together."

"Do you truly mean that?" Jayden asked.

"Yes." Myah said.

Jayden smiled and then he gave her a kiss.

"That's what I've been wanting the entire time." Jayden said.

The two of them continued their walk through the small village. Afterward, they went home and took care of Michael and spent time with him until he was about to fall asleep. Afterward, they went for a swim before they went inside and turned in for the night.

Chapter 12

The next day, as Jayden was looking for something in the refrigerator, he spotted something peculiar. He picked it up to get a closer look at it. Even though it was unusual, Jayden recognized it, and he suddenly became furious. In frustration, Jayden sighed, and then he put the fruit back into the refrigerator before he closed the door. Then he left the kitchen and stormed into the bedroom. Myah became nervous as Jayden entered the room. She could tell by the expression on his face that he was upset about something.

“Is everything alright?” Myah asked.

“How long has this been going on?” Jayden asked.

“What are you talking about?”

“When were you going to tell me?”

“Tell you what?”

“When were you going to tell me that the king was in the area?”

“Does it matter?”

“What do you think? Did you think that I’d be thrilled about it? I haven’t forgotten the fact that you had a crush on him.”

“No, but that’s all it was. I love you.”

"This is just great, and just when I thought that there was no one who would stand in my way."

"He's not standing in your way."

"He is! I can't ignore the fact that you had a crush on him."

"I'm with you. I love you. Why must we go through this again?"

"I can't stand the thought of him being here."

"But he's not even here."

"Oh no? Then explain this!" Jayden said.

He stormed out of the room, went into the kitchen, and took the fruit that he had spotted out of the refrigerator before he made his way back to the bedroom.

"I know for a fact that he's been here!" Jayden said.

"Jayden, you're overreacting." Myah said.

"He was here! This fruit came from him! I know it did!"

"He was only trying to help."

"I knew it!"

"Jayden, please, calm down. I told you that he was trying to help."

"Do you have his number?" Jayden asked.

Myah didn't respond.

"I want you to get on the phone and I want you to call him and tell him that he doesn't need to come here anymore! I'm the provider of this family, not him!" Jayden said.

"It's not necessary. I'll just email him."

"Have you been emailing him?"

"Yes, but it was because I was working for him. At first, I didn't know that he was the one who hired me."

"Well, there will be no more of that. You send him an email letting him know that you'll no longer be working for him, and he no longer needs to come around. After that, I better not ever catch you emailing or calling him." Jayden said.

Myah did as she was told while Jayden stood there and watched. He wanted to see to it that Endymion would get the message. Myah sent the message to Endymion to let him know that she wouldn't be working for him, and he didn't need to come around any longer. After she had finished, she stood up, looked at Jayden with an unhappy expression on her face, and then she shook her head.

"Are you happy now?" Myah askes.

“No.”

“He wasn’t even trying to come between us. Believe it or not, he cares about you.”

“So?”

“It’s true. It’s time that you knew the truth. He didn’t want me to tell you, but now, I don’t care, because you need to hear it.” Myah said.

“Oh, so you’ve been keeping secrets from me.”

“Yes, because you’re overly jealous, and he knows it.”

“I have every reason to be jealous.”

“He was doing nothing wrong. He was only trying to help, and he does care about you.” Myah said.

“I don’t believe you.”

"But it's true. Whenever he heard about what happened to you, he was devastated about it."

"I don't care. I don't want him here."

"Why? Why are you so bothered by him?" Myah asked.

"Did the flower in the kitchen come from him too?"

"Yes." Myah said.

Jayden became even more furious.

"It came from one of his tears." Myah said.

"Come again?"

"It's true. It fell into the flower pot when he was grieving."

"Yeah, right, and it conveniently fell into the flower pot."

"But it's true."

"Yeah? What was the crybaby grieving about?" Jayden asked.

"He was grieving over you."

"Do you really expect me to believe that?"

"I don't expect you to do anything."

"I still don't want him here."

"He wasn't trying to come between us. Furthermore, I'm not very happy with how you're acting right now. It speaks volumes about how much you don't trust me." Myah said.

She then got up and started to walk away.

"Don't you dare walk away from me!" Jayden said.

He then followed Myah into the living room.

"I said, don't walk away from me!" Jayden said.

"Maybe I want you to stop following me!" Myah said.

She then started back in the direction of the bedroom.

"Stop walking away from me!" Jayden said.

With an expression of anger on her face, Myah turned and looked at Jayden.

"By the way, he wasn't only trying to help me! He was also trying to help you! He really does care about you! If it wasn't for him, you wouldn't be here! He healed you, otherwise, you would've died in my arms. Maybe that's what you were trying to do. Was it?" Myah said.

With an angry expression still on her face, she shook her head, and then she stormed out of the room. She went back to the bedroom, and then she closed the door behind her.

Chapter 13

It wasn't long after Myah had gone into the room when the door came open and Jayden stepped into the room. He had an unhappy expression on his face as he looked at Myah.

"Why, Myah? Why did you walk away from me? I told you not to do that." Jayden said.

Myah wouldn't respond. She wouldn't even cast a glance at him.

"Are you seriously going to ignore me?" Jayden asked.

There was no response.

"Myah? Myah, please, talk to me. Say something." Jayden said.

A tear trickled down his face as he walked toward her. When he approached the bed, he broke down and wept. He sat down and covered his face with his hand as he cried.

"Please, don't shut me out. I love you and I don't want to lose you." Jayden said.

"I don't understand why you feel the need to get so upset. I'm not with him. I'm with you. He was only trying to help."

"We don't need his help."

"He cares about you."

"I can't ignore the fact that you had a thing for him. I also remember the fact that you danced with him at the party that was held for you."

"You weren't there."

"You also danced with Albert, and you wonder why I have a problem with other men coming around."

"Albert was just a friend."

"That's what they all say. Is it not?"

"I don't want to fight. If that's the reason you came into this room, then just stop. Just leave me alone."

"No! I'll never leave you alone!" Jayden said.

Tears ran down his face as he looked at Myah. He moved closer to her, but then she moved away from him.

"Myah, please, don't do this. You're hurting me. Stop breaking my heart." Jayden said.

He covered his face as he sobbed. Myah was about to get up when Jayden looked at her before he took hold of her hand.

"Don't walk away from me." he said.

He moved closer to her before he rested against her.

"Please, don't leave me." Jayden said.

As he closed his eyes, tears ran down his face.

"You can't blame me for being upset." Jayden said.

"I already told you that I love you. I made it clear that I wouldn't run anymore, yet you keep throwing the past in my face. How do you think that's supposed to make me feel? Have you once thought about that?" Myah said.

"Try thinking about how I feel. Imagine what it would be like to constantly be abandoned by people who were supposed to care. How would you like it if you loved someone, but were constantly being rejected by them? If that wasn't enough, think about what it would be like to have someone toy with your emotions. They give you the impression that they want to be with you, but then they turn around and decide to play this never-ending game of cat and mouse." Jayden said.

"That was never my intention. Why can't you see that?"

"I'm growing tired, Myah. To make things worse, you have men coming around, and you expect me to be okay with it."

"Maybe I'm growing tired. You have no idea how frustrating it is for me to have you keep bringing up the past. You do it all the time. You don't know when to stop. I've told you that I love you. I made it clear that I'd stay with you, yet it's never enough." Myah said.

She then got free from Jayden, and she got up.

"Where are you going?" Jayden asked.

Myah didn't respond as she left the room.

"Stop walking away from me!" Jayden said.

He then got up and followed Myah, who headed up to the trapdoor. When she approached it, she unlocked it, and then she left the underwater shelter. Myah went into one of the bedrooms and closed the door behind her. She walked over to the bed and sat down. It wasn't long until the door came open and Jayden stepped into the room. When he approached the bed, he sat down, but then Myah got up and left the room and went back down to the underwater shelter. Before Jayden had a chance to come down with her, Myah closed the trapdoor and locked it, preventing him from following her.

Chapter 14

Jayden became furious whenever he realized that Myah had locked the trapdoor. He thought for sure that Myah had broken her promise to him and was trying to escape him again. With an expression of fury on his face, Jayden stormed out of the house. He was about to dive into the water when suddenly, someone took hold of him by his shirt. He became confused when he suddenly noticed that his surroundings had changed.

"What's going on here?" Jayden asked.

As he glanced around, he became furious whenever he realized that he wasn't alone. He became even more enraged whenever he realized who it was that was with him.

"You! What have you done! Why did you bring me here!" Jayden said.

"It's nice to see you too, son." Endymion said.

"Stop calling me that! You're not my father!"

"I have something to say to you, and you better listen well to what I have to say."

"I don't have to listen to you."

"It would be wise if you did."

"I'd like to break every bone in your body!" Jayden said.

"That's enough!" Endymion said.

He had an expression of fury on his face as he looked Jayden in the eyes.

"I don't like how you've been talking to Myah. You've been treating her like garbage, and that's inexcusable. She doesn't need that. She deserves better than that." Endymion said.

"Shut your mouth, fool! You're the reason for the trouble!"

"Am I? You seem to be the one with the problem. Furthermore, you better cool it with the name-calling before I give you what you truly deserve.

"You don't scare me." Jayden said.

"I think it's time you grew up and take responsibility for your actions."

"And I think it's time for you to get a life and mind your own business."

"How long must you keep on with this little game of charades that you've been playing?"

"You don't know what you're talking about. Furthermore, I'd like to know why you've been hanging around my girl. Why can't you stay out of my life?"

"Why couldn't you stay where I put you? I was only trying to help you." Endymion said.

"I don't need your help! Leave me alone!"

"When are you going to go home and take care of your family?"

"I was home! You took me away from my family!"

"That's not what I meant, and I think you know that."

"It's none of your concern."

"I think it's time you get the help that you need instead of chasing after women. You need to take care of your family."

"I'm not chasing after women! I'm with one!"

"That wasn't the case not so long ago. You and I both know that." Endymion said.

"What I do is none of your business. Besides, you're probably not so innocent either."

"I know that we've been through this before, but I suppose that it didn't sink in."

"Whatever."

"Unlike you, I take responsibility for my actions. I try to improve the situation and I try to make better choices. What about you? You keep doing the same things over and over again and you expect to see different results."

"What are you implying?" Jayden asked.

"Do you really want me to answer that?"

"How about I knock your teeth out?"

"Don't even try it."

"Why can't you just stay away from me and my family?" Jayden asked.

"It's rather difficult whenever you act like a child, and you refuse to take responsibility for your family or your actions. It's truly a wonder I can get anything accomplished because anymore, it seems like all I get done doing is cleaning up your messes. I've lost count of the number of illegitimate sons of yours that I have to go around and take care of, not to mention the children who aren't illegitimate that you've chosen to ignore."

"I've never asked you to do that, in fact, I don't want you near any of my children, illegitimate or not."

"Somebody has to be a man and step up to take care of them. They need a father, and since you're too much of a child yourself, and you've decided not to, I've assumed that responsibility."

"You really think you're something."

"Why don't you come off your high horse before I knock you off of it."

"Stay out of my life!"

"Then grow up and get help!" Endymion said.

"I want to go home to my family."

"Myah doesn't even know who you are, not really. You have so much to hide from her. You masquerade as different individuals while you're at different locations. You've been living a double life, and you don't even use your real name. Do you even know who you are anymore? Meanwhile, Myah has no clue about who you truly are or what you've been doing." Endymion said.

"Stop it! Why can't you just let me be! I just want to live my life with my family. I love Myah and I want her to be a part of my life."

"Do you?"

"Yes!"

"What about that poor child that you continually abandon? He loves you, he needs you, and he cares about you, yet you don't care a thing about him. You continually abandon him and treat him like garbage."

"Stay out of my life!"

"You've treated him as a prisoner for no reason and without explanation. He deserves better than that." Endymion said.

"It's not your concern!"

"All he wants is your love and acceptance. He needs that, yet you refuse to give that to him. Does that sound familiar to you, son?"

"Stop calling me that!"

"Why won't you stop the vicious cycle that your father began? There needs to be a change, and it could begin with you."

"You don't understand."

"Why must you continue the vicious cycle? You're destroying your son's life."

"I've done nothing wrong."

"You have! You're just like your father; a lover boy who refuses to take responsibility for any consequence that follows. You won't bother to give your son, who's hurting, the one thing that he needs most. He thinks you hate him." Endymion said.

"Stop it!"

"What about Myah's son? What about the little ones that she's carrying now? Do you plan to mistreat them as well? Do you plan to imprison them as you do that precious child whom you continue to hurt? That's not a life for any of them, and they deserve better than that."

"I want you to take me home, and I want you to stay away from my family!"

"What about Myah? When are you going to tell her the truth? When are you going to stop yelling at her and stressing her out?"

"Stay out of my life!"

"She loves you. I know that for a fact. Are you even capable of loving anyone?"

"Leave me alone!" Jayden said.

Endymion sighed, and then he shook his head in disappointment as he kept his eyes on Jayden. Then he took him and teleported him back to where he had found him. Endymion said nothing more as he looked at Jayden one last time. He then shook his head before he vanished, leaving Jayden behind.

Chapter 15

Myah had just finished taking care of Michael, and he was about to fall asleep, so Myah took him to the crib and put him into it. She watched him as he drifted off to sleep. Then she left the room and went to her own room and sat down on the bed. She was still upset about the argument that she and Jayden had earlier. Myah put her hands on her face as she sat on the bed quietly. Then she laid down as she continued to think about what had happened. Suddenly, the door came open and Jayden stepped into the room with an angry expression on his face.

“Why did you lock me out!” Jayden said.

“I didn’t.”

“You locked the trapdoor.” Jayden said.

He got out of his wet clothes before he made his way over to the bed.

“I feel like you’re trying to push me away.” Jayden said.

“Why won’t you stop? Can’t you see that I don’t want to fight?”

“Do you even want to be with me?”

“I told you that I wanted to be with you, but I feel like I’m speaking to deaf ears. You refuse to listen to me.”

“I feel like you’re just with me because you want to keep Allen out of jail.”

"That's not true. I thought I had already made that clear?" Myah said.

Jayden said nothing as he looked at her sternly.

"I don't care if he goes to jail, in fact, Endymion already made it clear that Allen would get arrested if he found out that he was responsible for what happened to you."

"Oh, so now you're calling him by his name."

"What?"

"Do you have to keep talking about him?"

"I was just making a point. Believe it or not, he really does care about you, and he was very upset about what happened to you."

"Stop talking about him!" Jayden said.

Myah looked away from Jayden, who looked at her angrily.

"I can't do this anymore." Jayden said.

He then got up and left the room. He slammed the door, and then he left the underwater shelter. Myah sighed with relief because she couldn't stand Jayden yelling at her again.

Chapter 16

As time passed, Myah began to worry. It wasn't like him to be away for so long, especially since he was so adamant about being near her constantly. She decided to check on Michael, who was still asleep. Since Michael was asleep, Myah decided to search for Jayden. First, she went to the main house.

"Jayden?" she said.

She searched for him, but he was nowhere to be found. Myah began to worry more as she continued to search for him. Then she decided to go outside to search for him. She rushed outside and her heart sank whenever she spotted him face down and motionless in the water.

"No." Myah said.

Without hesitation, she dove into the water and swam toward him. When she approached him, she took hold of him and took him back to the house. Myah struggled to get Jayden onto the porch. She was devastated, for she feared that she had lost him. He wasn't breathing, and Myah broke down in tears. She checked for a pulse and when she realized that Jayden was still alive, she wasted no time. She acted quickly as she tried to revive him.

"Come on. Breathe." she said.

Jayden wouldn't respond, but Myah refused to give up. She didn't want to lose him again.

For a moment, it seemed hopeless, but then Jayden responded.

He coughed and then he spat water out. Jayden opened his eyes and looked right at Myah who broke down and wept. She took him in her arms and hugged him tightly as she cried. Jayden began to shiver, even as Myah hugged him. Then she looked at him before she got up. She helped him up and then the two of them went inside. She took Jayden to the bedroom and helped him over to the bed. He sat down and then Myah sat down beside him. Jayden looked at Myah before he moved closer to her. She hugged him tightly as his eyes welled up with tears as he rested against her. Myah hugged him even tighter as she thought about how close Jayden had come to dying again.

"Why?" Myah asked.

Jayden said nothing as he looked at Myah with tears running down his face.

"How could you do this? Why can't you just believe me whenever I tell you that I love you?" Myah asked.

Jayden covered his face as he wept.

"I thought I had lost you again." Myah said.

Tears filled her eyes as she looked at him.

"Don't ever do that again. Do you hear me? Don't do it." Myah said.

Tears ran down her face as she hugged him.

"I love you." she said.

Jayden said nothing as he rested against Myah as he wept. Myah didn't want to let him go after she had come so close to losing him for the second time.

Chapter 17

Several hours had passed since Myah had discovered Jayden unconscious in the water. For a while, everything was quiet as Jayden rested against Myah. Then suddenly, she heard Michael, and she got up, so she could see if he was okay.

"I'll be alright. I'm just going to check on Michael." Myah said.

She then gave Jayden a kiss before she left the room to check on Michael. Since he had awakened, she decided to take him upstairs so that he would be close by. Jayden watched

Myah as she entered the room with Michael. When she approached the bed, she sat down. Jayden remained quiet as he kept his eyes on Myah who took care of Michael. He moved closer to her, so he could rest against her. When Michael was about to fall asleep, Myah got up, took him to his room, and put him into his crib. Then she returned to the room and sat down beside Jayden, who snuggled up to her. He had the saddest expression on his face as he looked into Myah's eyes. Tears filled his eyes as he kept his eyes on her. Myah closed her eyes as she gave Jayden a kiss. Tears ran down his face as he looked at Myah, and then he closed his eyes as he kissed her. Then he rested against her once again.

"I've been thinking, and I've come to the realization that you must have wanted me to be here with you, otherwise you wouldn't have found me." Jayden said.

Then he sat up and looked into Myah's eyes.

"I'm very sorry." Jayden said.

"What were you thinking? You have so much to live for. Why would you do it?"

"I didn't think you cared."

"Of course I care. I've been telling you that, but you refuse to listen to me."

"Then are you willing to make it official?" Jayden asked.

"Are you talking about marriage?"

"Yes."

"Yes."

"Do you mean that?" Jayden asked.

"Yes, Jayden. I do." Myah said.

"Are you willing to relocate once more?"

"If that's what you want." Myah said.

Jayden looked into Myah's eyes as he spoke.

"I do." he said.

He gave her a kiss before he hugged her tightly.

"I'm glad that you're willing to do that for me because all the arrangements have already been made. I had already told you that I never planned to make this place our permanent home. Soon we'll be married and then, after that, we're going to leave this place, and we're going to go home." Jayden said.

He gave her another kiss, and then he sighed as he rested against Myah. At that moment, he was content because he felt that his troubles would finally come to an end.